Round the Turkey

A Grateful Thanksgiving

WRITTEN BY *Leslie Kimmelman*

ILLUSTRATED BY *Nancy Cote*

ALBERT WHITMAN & COMPANY

MORTON GROVE, ILLINOIS

To Ray, Natalie, and Greg, for whom
I am thankful each and every day.—L. K.

To Richard, Chris, Suzy, and Lizzie, for the
wonderful Thanksgiving memories.—N. C.

Library of Congress Cataloging-in-Publication Data

Kimmelman, Leslie.
Round the turkey : a grateful Thanksgiving / by Leslie Kimmelman ;
illustrated by Nancy Cote.
p. cm.
Summary: As they gather to celebrate Thanksgiving Day, members of an
extended family take turns describing, in rhyme, the things that make
them feel grateful.
ISBN 0-8075-7131-8 (hardcover)
[1. Thanksgiving Day — Fiction.
2. Family life — Fiction. 3. Stories in rhyme.]
I. Cote, Nancy, ill. II. Title. PZ8.3.K5598 Ro 2002
[E]--dc21 2002001957

For more information about Albert Whitman & Company,
please visit our web site at www.albertwhitman.com.

Mom

Dad

Peggy

Jonah

Jesse

Uncle Dave

Aunt Terry

Milo

Kaitlyn

My Turn (Jesse)

They're coming from near
and they're coming from far,
by plane and by train
and by bike and by car.
They can't wait to be
where the others all are—
everyone's coming to my house.

They're coming for turkey
and stuffing and pie,
for hugs and for kisses
and handshakes and "hi,"
for talking and laughing
till midnight goodbye—
my family, together, at my house!

Nana's Turn

It's Thanksgiving,
it's November.
Take a minute
to remember
all the blessings
of the year,
round the table,
starting here.

Aunt Terry's Turn

Our family had three:
it was Milo, Dave, and me.
We had love to spare,
so decided to share.

Now far away, waiting,
was our little Kaitlyn.
We flew through the night
and gathered her tight.

Mother

Father

Family

Brother

Uncle Dave's Turn

Today we are four,
and who could want more?

Kaitlyn's Turn

I like
my dog, Ike.

Ike's Turn

Woof woof
woof woof woof
woof woof drool
GRR
woof woof woof
slurp.

Psst. Want some turkey, Ike?

Milo's Turn

We had a school assembly
and everybody came:
the principal, the teachers,
and Mayor What's-His-Name.

We said the pledge of allegiance,
but that's not the whole story.
When it was time to sing some songs,
I got to hold Old Glory.

I didn't slouch or dip the flag;
I stood up straight and proud—
right through "God Bless America,"
the music growing loud.

We sang of purple majesties
and amber waves of grain.
We sang so loud they heard us down
on Fifty-first and Main.

Now others shared the stage with me,
and some made speeches, too.
But I'm the guy who held up high
the great red, white, and blue.

Carolyn's Turn

I climbed a tree
to save a cat.
My pants got torn.
I lost my hat.

I grabbed the cat
without a fight.
I slithered down
and held it tight.

And then, kaboom!
I slipped and fell.
I hit the ground
and gave a yell.

The ambulance
was really cool.
I got to miss
two days of school!

Can I sign your cast, Carolyn?
Sure, Jesse.

Nelson's Turn

Tina, Deena, Max, and Mike,
George the Third, Bernard, and Spike,
Woody, Wendell, Wanda Lee,
Genghis Khan and Dapper D.,
Molly, Lolly, Malcolm, Jim,
Gabe and Babe and Fats and Slim—
in my tanks, swim and swish,
lots of thanks for all my fish.

Hey, Nelson, we got you a new one for
Thanksgiving. His name is Pumpkin Pie.
Cool! Thanks, Jesse.

Thuthan'th (Susan's) Turn

Every Thaturday, all latht year,
I went to thee Mith Vandermeer.
My thpeaking thkillth were quite a meth;
Mith V. helped me with letter "eth."
I practithed hard, and finally,
"You've got it now!" Mith V. told me.
I feel tho proud, tho thatithfied,
I knew I'd get it if I tried.
"I think you need more work," you thay?
I lotht two teeth thith Thaturday.

Way to go, Susan!

Mark and Julie's Turn

Late for work.
> *Missed the train.*

Hole in sock.
> *Caught in rain.*

Coughed and sneezed.
> *Throat felt sore.*

Lost my watch.
> *How much more?*

Spilled my soup.
> *Spilled my tea.*

I looked up.
> *You saw me.*

THANKS!

Is Aunt Julie getting married again, Mom?

She sure is, Jesse.

Sophie's Turn

This is my brother, Jeffrey.
I'm thankful that he's here.
He's only been my brother
for one month and a year.
He learned his first word yesterday.
He's gonna say it now.
Okay, Jeffie, it's your turn.
Say the word, Jeff:
WOW.

He drools a bit; he sleeps too much—
but Jeffie, take a bow.
You'll just keep getting better.
The word for that is ...
WOW!

Uncle Hershey's Turn

Just a minute. I'm still chewing.
Okay, ready now.

Turkey with stuffing,
cranberry muffin,
ripe red tomatoes,
yams and potatoes,
succotash,
yellow squash,
beets,
sweets,
pumpkin pie,
my, oh, my.
Rub-a-dub-dub—
thanks for the grub!

Hey, Jesse, pass the gravy, will you?

Aunt Nina's Turn

Look, everyone—it's snowing!

Falling, dancing, soft-lace flakes
blanketing the world with white.
What could be as magical
as snowfall on Thanksgiving night?
Outside: hushed, enchanted land.
Inside: noisy, loving clan.
Falling, dancing, soft-lace flakes
blanketing the world with white.
First snow of the winter season—
thanks for such an awesome sight.

Peggy's Turn

Hiya, Zack.
Yeah, it's me.
Yakity-yak.
I agree.
Eight o'clock?
Yakity-yak.
I'll ask Jill.
Call me back.

Yo, it's me.
Yakity-yak.
Got a dress.
Pink and black.
Eight o'clock.
Meet out back.
See you then.
Yakity-yak.

Abby! Hey!
How was track?
Second place!
Yakity-yak.
Pretty mad.
Blew her stack.
Catch you later.
Yakity-yak.

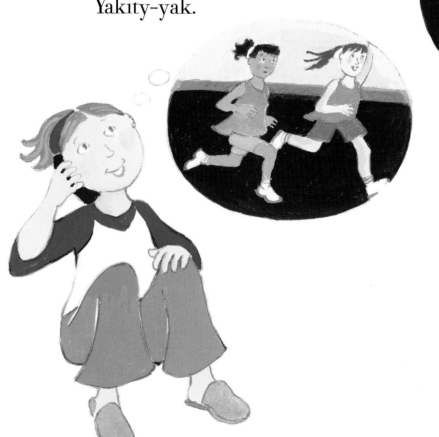

I'm thankful, you know,
for my new phone, see?
Briiing! *Gotta go.*
That's prob'ly for me!

Mom and Dad's Turn

Thanks for Peggy,
Jonah, Jesse—
sometimes loud
and sometimes messy;
sometimes pick
a silly fight;
sometimes up
too late at night;
rarely listen
when we call;
often drive us
up the wall.
But worry though we may about them,
watch our hair grow gray about them,
still, we'd like to say about them:
wouldn't want one day without them!

Jonah's Turn

Ninth inning,
loaded bases.
Two men out,
anxious faces.
Sweaty hands,
steady bat.
OUT
OF
THE
BALLPARK!
Thanks for that.

Grampa's Turn

Roof is holding.
Car still runs.
Got some hair left;
having fun.

Heart's a-beating,
hear just fine.
Lots of grandkids
to call mine.

So please pass me another plateful.
For this year, I'm truly grateful.

I love you, Grampa.
I love you too, Jesse.

My Turn (again)

This has been the best Thanksgiving ever.

Going home 'neath shining moon;
thank you, thank you—come back soon!